To **Archie**

For being good.
MERRY CHRISTMAS!

From

It was a crisp Christmas Eve
and Santa and his reindeers
were busy delivering presents to
all the good boys and girls.

Santa's sleigh zoomed over houses, twisting
and turning silently through the snowy night sky.
Santa squeezed down and up and up and down
chimneys, carefully and quietly delivering
lots of presents.

was going to ...lan until he reached the ...cond to last ...se on his list.

Suddenly, Santa realised one of the presents was missing!

The reindeer looked in Santa's sack, they searched everywhere but the present was nowhere to be found! "Oh no!" exclaimed Santa. "It must have fallen off the sleigh!"

5

Santa wondered what to do. He had no time to look for the present but he didn't want to disappoint anyone on his Christmas list.

Then Santa had a FANTASTIC idea!

Naughty & Nice LIST

He looked at his delivery map to see where they were. Then he checked his list to see who had been **naughty** or ni

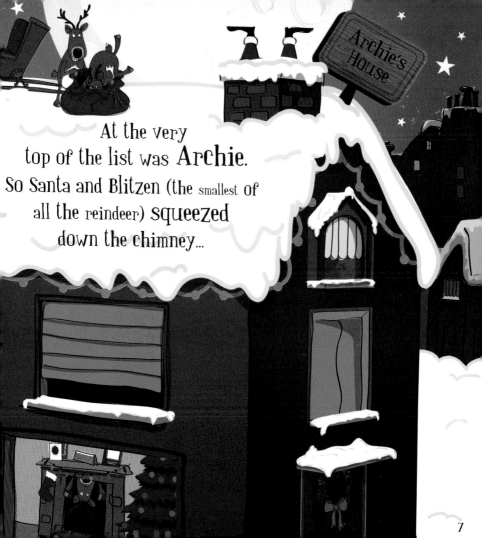

At the very
top of the list was **Archie**.
So Santa and Blitzen (the smallest of
all the reindeer) **squeezed**
down the chimney...

his

into

quietly

crept

...and

bedroom.

Archie yawned,
stretched and rubbed
his eyes. He thought he
was still dreaming until Blitzen licked his
face with his long, wet, pink tongue - YUCK!

8

"I need your help!" boomed Santa. He explained that a present had fallen off the sleigh and Santa wanted **Archie** to go with Blitzen to find it.

Archie of course was VERY happy to help.

9

It was cold and snowy outside so **Archie** put on his warmest hat and favourite stripy scarf.

Archie and Blitzen looked through Santa's telescope.

They looked down past the houses and through the trees, trying to find the lost present.

Suddenly they spotted it, sitting on top of a pile of snow at the bottom of a big hill.

He jumped on Blitzen's back and gave him a friendly pat and little tickle behind his fluffy ears. Then with a gentle nudge they flew high into the starry night sky.

Up and up they soared

and higher higher higher

until Blitzen did a
loop the loop,
a flip and a flop
and landed with a bop
next to the pile of snow...

but the present had gon

12

Archie and Blitzen looked around but couldn't see the present anywhere!

All of a sudden Blitzen's wet nose began to itch and itch and wibble and wobble. What had he found?

Archie saw a bright orange carrot sticking out of the snow. "Who likes carrots?" he wondered. Perhaps this was a clue to where the present had gone.

13

Then they saw a tiny white and grey bunny rab

"Hello Mrs Rabbit, we'r looking for a missing gift which fell from Santa's sleigh. Have you seen anything

The bunny twitched her nose, rubbed her ears and pointed a fluffy white paw at a line of acorns.

14

"Who likes acorns?"
wondered **Archie**.

Then looking down they noticed a
bouncy red squirrel staring back at them.
hey followed him, picking up the **acorns** one by one,
knowing who or what would be at the end of the trail.

15

As they picked up the final acorn,
they noticed a nose-less,
button-less, very sad snowman
right in front of them.

His carrot nose had fallen
off and his acorn
buttons had been
lost but there,
poking out fro
under his black ha
was a shiny
Christmas present

16

Hurray, they had found the present... but why did the snowman have it?

The sad snowman explained that every year he felt forgotten as he never received a present. When he found this one he was so happy. However, now he knew it belonged to someone else, he wanted to give it back.

17

Feeling sorry for the snowman,
Archie decided to help.
He placed the half-eaten **carrot**
on the snowman's face for his nose
and the **acorn** buttons on his body
but the snowman still looked sad.

Then **Archie**
had a brilliant idea!

He undid his favourite woolly scarf and tied it around the surprised snowman.

Then he replaced the snowman's old black hat with his warm knitted one.

The snowman was so happy! At last he had his very OWN Christmas present!

Archie and Blitzen flew as fast as they could to get the missing present back in time for Christmas morning.

Archie placed the gift under the tree with a huge sigh of relief!

Back at home Archie gave Blitzen a big hug, then watched as his new friend flew up into the sky and home to Santa.

When **Archie** woke up on Christmas morning, he wondered if it had all been a dream. Then he looked out of his window...

...and there in the distance was the **happy** snowman waving at him and he was still wearing his **lovely** Christmas present.

The end

21